Mr. Doodle
Had a Poodle

Do you know . . .

A library is a magic castle with many Word Windows in it?

What is a Word Window?

If you answered, "A book," you're right.

A book is a Word Window because the words, and the pictures that tell about the words, let you look and see many things. Books are your windows to the wide, wide world around you.

CHILDRENS PRESS
HARDCOVER EDITION
ISBN 0-516-05728-6

CHILDRENS PRESS
PAPERBACK EDITION
ISBN 0-516-45728-4

Library of Congress Cataloging in Publication Data

Moncure, Jane Belk.
    Mr. Doodle had a poodle.

  (Magic castle readers)
    Summary: Even though he has not quite mastered
the skill of barking, Mr. Doodle's poodle performs
many tricks. Includes a vocabulary list.
    [1. Dogs—Fiction.   2. Vocabulary]   I. Hohag,
Linda, ill.   II. Title.   III. Series: Moncure,
Jane Belk.   Magic castle readers.
PZ7.M739Mr   1988   [E]   87-15808
ISBN 0-89565-409-1

Mr. Doodle Had a Poodle

by Jane Belk Moncure
illustrated by Linda Hohag

Created by  THE CHILD'S WORLD

Distributed by CHILDRENS PRESS®
Chicago, Illinois

The Library — A Magic Castle

Come to the magic castle
When you are growing tall.
Rows upon rows of Word Windows
Line every single wall.
They reach up high,
As high as the sky,
And you want to open them all.
For every time you open one,
A new adventure has begun.

Jeff opened a Word Window.
Guess what Jeff saw?

Mr. Doodle with a poodle.

Mr. Doodle was trying to get
his poodle to bark.

The poodle would dance and hop
and skip. She would even . . .

do a flip. But Mr. Doodle's poodle
would not bark.

She would jump rope.

She would ski. She would . . .

climb the apple tree. But Mr. Doodle's
poodle would not bark.

She would swim.

She would dive.

She would count from one to five. But
Mr. Doodle's poodle would not bark.

She would read books.

She would write. She liked to write.

She would even fly a kite.

She would skate and . . .

drive a car.

She would play a big guitar. But
Mr. Doodle's poodle would not bark.

She would cut the grass . . .

and rake.

She would even bake a cake.
But would she bark? Oh no.

She would sing a happy song. . . . "Happy Birthday to you. Happy Birthday to you."

She would even play ping-pong. But
Mr. Doodle's poodle would not bark.

Then one evening on a walk, she met a cat. The cat said, "Meow," and . . .

Mr. Doodle's poodle said, "Bow-wow."

So Mr. Doodle's poodle did know how.

What are some funny things Mr. Doodle's poodle would do?

dance

jump rope

do a flip

ski

climb a tree

swim

skate

read
a
book

count to five

fly
a
kite

bake
a
cake

Now you make up more funny things a
silly poodle might do.